Big Shark, Little Shark, Baby Shark

by Anna Membrino
illustrated by Tim Budgen

Random House 🏠 New York

Big shark.

Little shark.

Big Shark and
Little Shark are friends.

They are at the
Shark Park.

They play games.
They have fun!

9

Oh no.

Here comes

Baby Shark.

Big Shark and
Little Shark
do NOT want to play
with Baby Shark.

Baby Shark
is too little.
Baby Shark
is too slow.

It is NOT fun
to play with
Baby Shark!

Big Shark and
Little Shark

swim away.

Baby Shark is sad.

Baby Shark swims
to Mommy Shark
and Daddy Shark.

They are mad
at Big Shark and
Little Shark.

Mommy Shark tells
Grandpa Shark
what Big Shark
and Little Shark did.

Grandpa Shark tells
Grandma Shark
what Big Shark
and Little Shark did.

The family of sharks
is mad!

What will they do?

All five sharks
take a deep breath.

They will play
their own game!

28

Now Big Shark
and Little Shark
want to play!

They say
they are sorry
for not being kind.

Baby Shark
asks them to play, too.

They all play
shark baseball
together!

32